Marshall Cavendish Corporation
99 White Plains Road, Tarrytown, NY 10591
www.marshallcavendish.us/kids

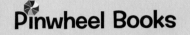

# Pinwheel Books

Library of Congress Cataloging-in-Publication Data

Olson, Julie, 1976–
 Tickle, tickle! itch, twitch! / Julie Olson. — 1st ed.
  p. cm.
 Summary: Gus the groundhog desperately needs
to scratch his back after a mouse tickles him with a
feather, but the stick, bush, and log he tries to scratch
against are not what they appear to be.
   ISBN 978-0-7614-5714-5
 [1. Itching—Fiction. 2. Woodchuck—Fiction. 3. Animals—
Fiction.] I. Title.
 PZ7.O5212Tic 2010      [E]—dc22      2009030269

The illustrations are rendered in watercolor
and digital media.

Book design by Vera Soki
Editor: Nathalie Le Du

Printed in Malaysia (T)
First Marshall Cavendish Pinwheel Books edition, 2010
1 3 5 6 4 2

**mc Marshall Cavendish**
Children

# Tickle, Tickle! Itch, Twitch!

written and illustrated by
## Julie Olson

Marshall Cavendish Children

For Rhett and Spencer,
who always need their backs scratched
—J.O.

**G**us loved lazy summer days—
picking daisies, sleeping in the
shade, watching the clouds go by.

But one afternoon . . .

Tickle, tickle!

Itch, twitch!

Gus grabbed a stick,
reached back to scratch, and . . .

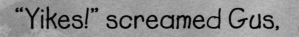

Hisssssssssssssss

"Yikes!" screamed Gus,

and away he ran.

"That was a close one," Gus said.
But then . . .

Tickle, tickle!

Gus ran to a spiky bush, backed up
to rub against it, and . . .

until he could run no more. "I'm going
to get poked, bit, and eaten, but I've . . .

gotta, gotta, gotta, gotta, gotta . . .

Gus looked around for something
to scratch the itch, when . . . Oh NO!

Gus ran for his life . . .

He pulled himself out of the water and collapsed. "I don't think I can take anymore," and then . . . there it was again!

Tickle, tickle! Itch, twitch!

# SNAP!

It wasn't a log at all.
Gus rolled off and fell into the river.

Gus spotted a log, wiggled on top of it, and . . .

# Pi-inggggg!

"YEOOOW!" Gus hopped in the other direction.

"Whew!" he sighed. But then . . .

Tickle, tickle!
Itch, twitch!

Oh no!
"Gotta, gotta, gotta scratch
my BAA-AA-ACK!"
yelled Gus.